Mystery
of the
Golden
Temple

Mystery
of the
Golden
Temple

BY LISA TRAVIS

ILLUSTRATIONS BY ADAM TURNER

Published by WorldTrek Publishing

Printed in the USA

Visit our website at www.packngogirls.com.

This is a work of fiction. Names, characters, places, and incidents either are the product of the author's imagination or are used fictitiously. The city of Chiang Mai, Thailand, is real, and it's a wonderful place to visit. Any other resemblance to actual events, locales, organizations, or persons, living or dead, is entirely coincidental and beyond the intent of either the author or the publisher.

Illustrations by Adam Turner

ISBN 978-1-936376-09-4

Cataloging-in-Publication Data available from the Library of Congress.

To Mom and Dad, who inspired my entrepreneurial and adventurous mindset.

Contents

Meet the Characters

Jess Johnson loves playing soccer almost as much as mysterious adventures in faraway places.

Jared Johnson is Jess' older brother. He likes karate and dirt biking. He keeps an eye on his little sister too.

Nong May Wattana likes to sing, dance, and make new friends. She is excited to show her new friend, Jess, all around Chiang Mai.

Pee Aran Wattana is Nong May's older brother. He likes Muay Thai (Thai boxing) and works at the Elephant Rescue Center.

NOTE: Nong May and Pee Aran speak some Thai in this book. Use the language glossary on page 98 to learn how to pronounce Thai. To keep things simpler for readers, tonal marks are not used in the text.

The Golden Temple
is hidden somewhere!

And now, the mystery begins . . .

Mystery of the Golden Temple

Chapter 1

Off to a Faraway Place

Jessica Johnson knew the drill. Shoes off. Jacket off.
No water. Put your bag on the moving belt-thingee.
And don't forget to give them your favorite stuffed
puppy, Pink Dog. It didn't matter that her favorite
stuffed animal had been through the moving belt
machine-thingee a gazillion times, Jess still worried a
little. What if THIS time she didn't come out on the
other end?

The officer motioned Jess to step through the

metal arch. He glanced up at the top. "Step aside and wait here, please." The man smiled and nodded in the direction he wanted her to go. She already knew she needed to wait for her mom. It was all part of the drill.

Jess fidgeted with her favorite soccer ball necklace while she waited. She craned her neck to see the other end of the moving belt thingee. Pink fluff crushed up against someone else's suitcase at the end. Now she had to worry that someone would see how cute Pink Dog was and take her. No one ever did, but what if THIS time someone did?

Airport security? A major drag.

Thank goodness her mom stepped through the arch at that moment. They gathered their stuff off the belt-thingee. Jess grabbed Pink Dog and hugged her big time.

This trip was the farthest away from home Jess had ever been. Her mom had showed her Thailand on their globe. She couldn't believe it was on the other side of the planet. Her mom said they'd see golden palaces and temples and jungles. They might even get to see some elephants.

Jess couldn't stop wondering about so many things. "Are the people in Thailand nice?" she asked her mom. "Do they speak English? Do I have to eat anything weird?"

"Jess, the food in another country is not 'weird.' It's just different from ours. Don't worry about it. You'll be just fine," Mrs. Johnson said.

Just fine. Oh yeah. Jess had heard that one about a million times. In her nine short years, Jess had been "just fine" in over ten different countries already. And it wasn't always "just fine."

Like the time they bought the wrong tickets for the ferry in Greece. They had to sleep all night on hard benches instead of cushy seats.

Not just fine.

Or the time it took ten hours to go 200 miles on a winding, dusty road in Peru.

Definitely NOT just fine.

But that's what you get when your parents like to work with schools around the world.

"Group one can now board. Group one only."

"That's us," Mr. Johnson said.

"Me first," Jess' older brother, Jared, said as he slyly stepped in front of her.

Jess knew why. They both wanted the window seat so they could watch the plane take off and see the land disappear below them. Totally cool.

"Hey—that's not fair," Jess said in her loudest inside voice. "It's my turn to have the window seat."

"You snooze you lose," Jared said.

"Stop, *please*," Mrs. Johnson said in *her* loudest inside voice. "We've got a long trip ahead of us. Jess, you get the window to London. Jared, you can ride in the window seat from London to Bangkok."

Off to a Faraway Place

"Bangkok?" Jess asked.

"That's the capital city of Thailand. After we land in Bangkok, we'll switch planes one more time to Chiang Mai, which is in northern Thailand."

"Chang My?" Jess said, trying hard to say it right. "Geeeesh. How long is this going to take?"

"Probably a little over one full day and night," Mr. Johnson said.

"What? We're going to travel all day and all night? Seriously? You didn't tell us it would be *this* long! This is going to take for-*ever*."

"Jessica, now is not the time to start whining. You'll be just fine," Jess' mom said again as they boarded the plane.

After a very, very, *very* long time—on the afternoon of the next day to be exact—Jess stumbled off the plane in Chiang Mai, Thailand. The first thing she noticed was the strange letters:

ท่าอากาศยานเชียงใหม่

Jess tugged at her mom's arm. "Mom, Mom, Mom—is that the language here? Why is it so swirly? What does it say?"

"Jess, Jess, Jess," Mrs. Johnson teased. "Yes, that's their language. They speak Thai here. It sounds like T-I-E, but it is spelled T-H-A-I, like the first part of Thailand. But you can look below and see the words in English: Chiang Mai International Airport. Let's hurry along now, we've got to catch a taxi."

The taxi driver zoomed wildly out of the airport. Jess decided this was not like a taxi in Boston or even New York. Not only was he driving all crazy, the inside was decorated all crazy. Necklaces with little square charms hung from the mirror. Golden coins and statues were glued all over the dashboard. And pictures of royal looking people were taped up on the car seats and roof.

Jess leaned over to her mom and whispered, "Who are they?"

"Oh, that is His Majesty the King of Thailand and his wife, the Queen. They are very loved here in Thai—"

Just then a motorbike zipped out in front of them. The taxi swerved and the driver slammed on his brakes. One of the statues flew off the dashboard straight at Jess. It crashed on the floor and splintered into a million pieces.

Nearly in tears, the driver mumbled in a mix of Thai and English, "No, no, no . . . bad luck." He suddenly skidded to a stop on the side of the road.

Jess thanked her lucky stars to be safe. Seemed like good luck to her.

"Bad luck. It broken," the taxi driver cried. He frantically waved them out of the car. "Keep driving . . . be very bad luck. Get out here."

The whole family sat, frozen. Did he just say to get out?

"Get out here. Please get out," he repeated. "Bad luck. Go. Go. GO!"

He pushed the Johnsons out of the car. Then he sped away leaving them and their bags on the street.

"Don't worry, guys," Mr. Johnson said. He shook his head and rubbed his neck. "We'll be just fine."

Definitely and totally NOT just fine.

Chapter 2

Bad Luck

"Why did he just leave us here on the street? What did he mean by bad luck? Who—"

"Jess, enough with the questions," Mr. Johnson said. He sighed. "I said we would be just fine. And we will. Look at that. Here comes a taxi now." He waved at the taxi. When the taxi stopped, Mr. Johnson poked his head in the window. "Do you speak English?" he asked.

The taxi driver smiled and nodded politely but

did not reply out loud. They loaded their bags into the trunk and stuffed themselves into the small car.

"We are headed to the Thai Garden Guesthouse in the Mae Sa Valley. It's on Route 1096. Do you know where that is?"

Once again, the taxi driver smiled and nodded but did not reply.

Coins, pins, and charms completely covered the dashboard. Some overflowed on to the roof. Three bobbleheads happily bobbed their heads back and forth. A picture of His Majesty the King swung from the mirror as they drove. Jess noticed a card taped to the dashboard that showed the driver's picture and name: Mr. Somwan.

I hope Mr. Somwan can get us to our guesthouse Jess thought to herself. Did he really speak English? She hadn't heard him say anything in English yet. What if they spent 20 MORE hours driving around and around Thailand? With bad luck, maybe they would NEVER get there.

But they did get there. Finally. The sight of lush green trees greeted Jess when she stepped out of the taxi. Neat little paths curved around to the small red guesthouses that dotted the hillside. Red, yellow, and orange flowers bloomed next to a flowing stream. And the pink flowers. Oh, the amazing pink flowers! Jess breathed in the sweet scent and sighed a happy (but tired) sigh. She had arrived at a garden paradise, and she couldn't wait to explore.

But first, she really had to go to sleep. She unpacked and flopped on her bed.

"Jess, what are you doing?" her mom asked. "You can't sleep now."

"What do you mean I can't sleep? I've been up for a gazillion hours. I'm tired. I want to sleep." It was time for bed.

Only it wasn't.

"I'm sorry, but you can't go to sleep now, or you

will wake up in the middle of the night. You need to stay up a little later so you can get used to Thai time."

"Thai time? That's a tongue twister," Jess murmured. She closed her eyes. "I'm just going to take a little nap."

"No you're not. Let's go over and meet Khun Mali. She has a little girl your age and a boy Jared's age. I am sure playing with them will keep you both awake."

"Koon who?" Jared asked.

"Khun Mali. It's like saying Mrs. Molly in English. In Thailand, they use *Khun* to show respect like we use Mrs. in the States. What's different is that we use *last* names afterwards, like Mrs. Johnson or your friend's mother, Mrs. Clark. The Thai people use *first* names afterwards. They will call me Khun Jayla. Got it?" Mrs. Johnson nodded her head, raised her eyebrows, and waited for a response.

"Yup, we got it," Jared said.

Bad Luck

They wound their way through a twisty path to the orchid farm next door. The tree branches over their heads created a jungle-like feel.

"I have been working with Khun Mali to help schools in the nearby hill tribe villages," Mrs. Johnson said as they walked. "Her husband's family has owned this small orchid farm for years. They ship their rare orchid flowers all over the world."

They found themselves in front of a beautiful old wooden house with a peaked roof and a wide porch. They climbed the steps to the front door and knocked.

A slight woman answered the door.

"*Sawatdee kha*, Khun Jayla. Hello. Welcome to Thailand," the woman said. She placed the palms of her hands together at the center of her chest. Her hands titled outward as she bowed her head. Her index fingers touched her nose. Mrs. Johnson returned the bow.

"Jess, Jared, you can do the same and say sa-wat-dee," Mrs. Johnson said. "Oh, and Jess, because you're a girl, you should add *kha* at the end. Jared, men add *khrap* to the end."

Jess tilted her head. "Huh?"

Her mom smiled. "This is saying hello. The bow is called a *wai*. Together they are the formal way to greet people in Thailand."

"Um . . . okay . . . *Sawatdee kha*," Jess said with a smile and a bow.

A happy round face peered around the corner. Khun Mali spoke quickly in Thai. A slender girl walked over to them and bowed. She bowed a little lower than her mother. Her thumbs touched her nose and her index fingers touched between her eyebrows. Jess wondered if she was supposed to do it that way too.

"*Sawatdee kha. Di-chan cheu Nong May kha.* Hello. My name is Nong May." Her mouth was shaped into a sweet smile that turned up at the corners. Playful eyes peered through her hair. Then she covered her mouth and giggled.

Jess wasn't sure what she was laughing at, but she knew she would like her. She looked different than Jess, but somehow a lot the same. Both girls had big brown eyes, brown skin, and brown hair. Nong May had lighter skin and wispy, stick-straight, short hair

that framed her face. Jess had darker skin and thick dark brown hair all done in tiny braids. Nong May was smaller and skinnier than Jess, who had a more athletic build. But they both looked ready to play.

"I must bring dinner over to Khun Yaa, my grandmother. Do you want to go?" asked Nong May.

"Sure," Jess said. A wide smile spread across her face. "Can I go, Mom?"

"Of course. I have some work to do with Khun Mali. Stay awake!"

"So how did you learn to speak English?" Jess asked as they walked away.

"I learn it at school. And my mother does a lot of work with English-speaking people. So one of her friends comes to teach me too."

"Wow. Your English is really good. I don't know any Thai."

"Then I can teach you some."

Bad Luck

"What are all these flowers hanging from the roof?" Jess asked. They walked through row after row of blooming flowers with long stems. Soft, velvety petals in purples, pinks, oranges, reds—almost every color actually—surrounded them. Butterflies fluttered here and there among the blossoms.

"These are the orchids we grow here. My father runs this farm."

"Every color of the rainbow must be hanging in here," Jess said. "It must be really awesome to wander through these orchids every day. I bet they make you soooo happy all the time."

"Well, the orchids are pretty. I wish they could bring us more happiness though," Nong May said. She looked sad all of a sudden.

"Why are you and your family not happy? This farm is beautiful."

"Yes, it is. But it has been hard for my family

since we lost our ancient *Phra Somdej Wat Rakhang*," Nong May said. Her shoulders sagged.

"Pra-someday-what-thingee?" Jess' tongue twisted around the words.

"It is a powerful, how do you say . . . thing that protects us from harm and brings us good fortune."

"I think I heard of something like that. My favorite cartoon in America, *Scooby Doo*, had an amulet in it. Daphne wore it. It glowed and had special powers. Is it something like that?"

"Yes. That must be the English word for it— amulet. Our amulet does not glow, but our family thinks it has special powers," Nong May said. "*Wat Rakhang* is the temple where it was made. The great monk Somdej Toh made amulets in the late 1800s to give good fortune to the world. People who have these amulets receive many blessings because Somdej Toh was not selfish when he made them."

"So did this Somdej Toh really make *your*

18

amulet?" Jess asked.

"Yes. Not many people in Thailand have such an old amulet from the temple where Somdej Toh made them. It has been passed down in our family for generations. Today, our amulet would be worth millions of baht."

"Millions? Wow!" Jess thought about what that meant in dollars. But that was way too hard of a math problem to do in her head.

Guessing what Jess was trying to figure out, Nong May said, "I heard my dad tell my mom that it was worth more than $100,000 in your money."

"$100,000?" Jess' eyes widened. "So your family lost all of that money? No wonder you're not happy."

"Yes, but it is not the money. Even if we had it, we would not sell it." Nong May's eyes shifted down to the floor. "When we had the *Phra Somdej*, we were blessed." She looked at Jess and sighed. "Since we lost it, bad luck has come our way. Lots of bad luck."

A shiver shot up Jess' spine. Uh-oh. There it was again. Bad luck.

Chapter 3

The Missing Amulet

As they rounded the corner, they saw Khun Yaa sitting on the porch of her house in a rocking chair. A smile spread across her face as she spoke to Nong May.

To Jess, the Thai language sounded like they were singing to each other. Their voices went up and down and up and down some more.

"She wants to know all about you, Jess," Nong May said.

"*Sawatdee kha*, Khun Yaa," Jess said with a bow. She was careful to copy how Nong May had done it before. "*Di-chan cheu Jess kha*," Jess said. Hello, Khun Yaa. My name is Jess. She bit her lip nervously. Trying to practice the tiny bit of Thai Nong May had just taught her was a little scary. Did she get it right?

"*Sawatdee kha*, Nong Jess," Khun Yaa replied.

Jess turned quickly to Nong May, "Why did she call me *Nong* Jess? Isn't *Nong* part of *your* name?"

"Oh, we use *Nong* to mean 'little,' like little sister. When we talk to people younger than us, we use *Nong* before their

22

name. I am the youngest in my family, so they all call me Nong May. When we talk to people older than us, we use *Pee*. That means older. My brother is older than me, so I call him Pee Aran."

"*Pee*, really?" Jess held back a laugh and kept her bathroom jokes to herself. She knew better than to laugh at how people say and do things in another country. She turned to Khun Yaa and politely answered her question while Nong May translated what she said.

"Well, I am from Boston, Massachusetts, which is a small state in the northeast part of the United States. I am nine-years old. My favorite color is green. And I like to sing and play soccer," Jess said. She held out her favorite soccer ball necklace from around her neck for Khun Yaa to see.

"*Jeng*! Awesome," Nong May said. Her eyes brightened with excitement.

"I like to sing too, and *my* favorite color is green.

Like the jungle."

"Wow! I guess even on the other side of the world, we can have some things that are the same."

They sat on the porch and talked with Khun Yaa. Jess thought back to her conversation with Nong May. She couldn't stop wondering about the amulet. How did it get lost? When did this happen? Questions swirled in her head. Why was it bad luck? How could they find it? She couldn't hold back her questions any longer.

"So how did you lose the pra-someday-what amulet?"

"Since you are learning Thai, try to say it, Jess. Pra some-det. You end it with a quick, hard 'T' sound. But leave your tongue at the top of your mouth a little longer to make a breathy sound at the end."

Jess tried again, "Pra some-det." She was a little embarrassed trying to pronounce Thai. Her mom had told her that in English a word is a word. But in Thailand a word can change its meaning depending on the tone of voice. Not just one or two tones. Five different tones to be exact. She had shared the example that when she tried to say beautiful, she said unlucky instead. Whoops. She had used the wrong tone. That made Thai a hard language to speak. Jess knew she probably wasn't using her tone correctly. Oh boy. Well, at least she was trying.

"Yes, that's close," Nong May said. She covered her mouth and giggled.

Jess figured she probably did sound funny.

"Anyway, Khun Yaa can best answer your question," Nong May said.

Khun Yaa did not know English, so Nong May did her best to tell Jess what she said in English.

"For many years, the farm produced lots of orchids. The money we made took care of our family. My grandfather, Khun Pu, was even able to grow a very rare type of orchid. It was more beautiful than you can imagine."

Khun Yaa said something in Thai. Nong May nodded to her grandmother. "Then five years ago, we heard there were thieves and robbers coming into the Mae Sa Valley at night. The robbers attacked the farm down the road and stole most of their valuables."

"That stinks!" Jess exclaimed.

Nong May looked puzzled. "Well, it did not smell."

"I mean, that's terrible. Stinks means something is bad," Jess explained.

"Ohhhh, yes. It *was* terrible. Khun Pu, my grandfather, was very worried. He sent us all to stay with a friend in Chiang Mai the next night. But he stayed behind. When we came back, he was gone. And so was the *Phra Somdej* amulet."

"Did the robbers steal your stuff? What

happened to your grandfather?" Jess asked.

"Well, we never found the amulet, but my grandfather finally came back about three days later. He had a very high fever, and he was very confused. He kept talking about a golden temple in the jungle. A few days later, he died."

"Oh no. I am so sorry," Jess whispered quietly. She was also sorry she asked so many questions.

"Thank you," Nong May said. Her eyes watered up. The girls sat quietly for a minute. "Ever since then, we have had bad luck. My grandfather's rare orchids have not bloomed. And one of the main companies that bought our orchids decided to buy from Singapore. If we don't have a better year, we will have to sell our farm."

"That's terrible."

"Yes. It is very sad." Nong May got up, took off her shoes at the door, and slowly walked into her grandmother's house.

Jess' shoulders drooped. Why did she always have to ask so many questions? Why hadn't she learned to keep her mouth shut?

And there I go again, she thought to herself. Always more questions. Would Nong May even want to be her friend anymore? No one to play with in a faraway place?

That would be even more bad luck.

Chapter 4

The Broken Buddha

Jess copied Nong May and took off her shoes at the door. She remembered now what her mother had told her. It was disrespectful to wear shoes inside someone's home in Thailand. Her feet felt cool on the clean tile floor. She followed Nong May inside and watched her prepare her grandmother's dinner.

Khun Yaa's house smelled like a mix of the jungle outside and the yummy food Nong May brought over. Large wooden windows lined the walls on one side. The shutters opened up to the warm outside air. Dark wood paneling covered the other walls all the way up to the ceiling. A giant tree-like plant filled the corner of the room. The house felt open and airy but cozy at the same time.

A black antique-looking bookcase with a glass door on it stood against the wood-paneled wall. Inside, the books were stacked every which way on top of one another. Some had their spines showing and some had the pages showing. A gold swirly flower and leaf pattern decorated the outside. The top of the bookcase displayed more than ten golden statues like ones in the taxi. A picture of His Royal Majesty the King hung above the bookcase.

Jess wandered over to take a closer look.

"Those are our treasured family Buddhas," Nong May said.

"What are Boo-duhs?" Jess asked before she

could stop herself from asking another question.

"The statues are of Buddha. Buddha saw the truth about what the world is like. Buddha teaches us to give to others and to avoid doing anything that can hurt others. He teaches us to pay attention to our thoughts and actions. The statues are symbols that help us remember to have these good qualities, the qualities of Buddha—"

"Acccckkkkkk!" Jess screamed. A fast, yellow snake popped out from the plant in the corner and quickly slithered its way out the door. Jess scrambled up on a chair. Her left arm flew out behind her to keep her balance. Down crashed one of the Buddhas from the top of the bookcase.

"Oh, no! No . . . no . . . no . . ." Jess cried under her breath. Not more bad luck.

Nong May froze. She stared out the door. Her mouth flew wide open in surprise. Then her eyes shifted down to the broken Buddha.

"More bad luck . . . more bad luck . . ." Jess mumbled. She tried to pick up the pieces. Tears streamed down her face.

"*Mai pen rai.* It is okay, Jess. We have many Buddhas. Everything is okay. Don't worry," Nong May said with a polite smile and a soft laugh.

Jess crinkled her eyebrows in confusion. "But, but, but this is one of your family treasures. You don't need to lose another one. I'm so sorry. I'm so sorry . . ."

Nong May kneeled down to help pick up the pieces. "Jess, it is okay. No prob—

Wait. What's this?" Nong May said. She picked up a folded piece of paper.

She opened it and gasped.

"What? What? What is it?"

"It is a *wat*," Nong May said.

"A what?"

"A *wat*. A temple. A temple I have not seen before."

Jess leaned over Nong May's shoulder to look at the paper. She whispered under her breath, "It's not just any temple. It's the *golden* temple."

Chapter 5

"Wat" Could It Be?

Jess tossed and turned most of the night. She rolled over and opened her eyes. She hugged Pink Dog as the bright sun greeted her through the window. At first she wasn't sure where she was. Then she remembered she was on the other side of the world in Thailand.

"Hey, sleepy head," Mrs. Johnson said. "How did you sleep?"

"Ah, not so great. I kept waking up."

"Wat" Could It Be?

"That's because your body thinks night is day. It is 13 hours later than home. So, at night, your body thinks it is daytime. And during the day, it thinks it is nighttime."

"Aarrrrgggghhhh," Jess yawned. She stretched her arms above her head.

"Jess, you need to get up and get dressed. We are going into Chiang Mai today. Khun Mali and I are meeting some people who may donate some money to the hill tribe village schools. Your father is helping Nong May's father at the orchid farm. And Jared is going to help Nong May's brother at the Elephant Rescue Center. So we thought we would bring you girls along and then do something fun this afternoon."

A face appeared at the open door. "*Sawatdee kha*, Khun Jayla and Jess. It is time to go," Nong May said.

They drove out of the valley. Jess leaned over to Nong May, "So did you look at the picture of the golden temple again? Have you figured out where it is?"

"No. I showed it to my mom. She said, 'Oh, that's a nice drawing.'" Nong May whispered and imitated her mom. "I tried to explain, but she just told me I had a great imagination." Nong May sighed. "Maybe we can ask our moms to take us to *Wat Phra That Doi Suthep* later."

"To what pra what?"

"To Doy Soo-tep." Nong May said it slowly so Jess could repeat it.

"It is the most famous temple in Chiang Mai. They say it was built over 500 years ago," Nong May said. She leaned closer to Jess. "We call it *Doi Suthep* for short. Someone there *must* know this golden temple."

Jess thought about Nong May's plan as they arrived at the field office. While they waited and waited and waited, they played dolls. Jess' doll was the world famous singer, Gina. And Nong May's doll was the *other* world famous singer, Madee. In between songs, they talked about their plan to ask people about the golden temple.

Just as they thought they would break the *Guinness Book of World Records* for waiting, their moms came in.

"We thought we would take you girls to the zoo this afternoon since you have been so good this morning," Mrs. Johnson said.

"Actually, Mom, can we go see *Doi Suthep*?" Jess asked.

Mrs. Johnson and Khun Mali looked at each other, puzzled.

"You want to go to the temple instead of the zoo?" Mrs. Johnson asked. She raised her eyebrows.

The two girls looked at each other. Then Jess turned to her mom with her best good-girl look, "Um, yes . . . Nong May said it was really, really beautiful. Please?"

"Well, okay then." They hopped in their car, zoomed past the zoo, and headed up the mountain to *Doi Suthep*.

When they reached the top of the mountain, they all got out of the car. Jess looked up, up, and up.

She stared at the 306 stone steps that led up to the temple. Trees lined each side, creating what looked like a narrow stairway. On both sides of the steps, a seven-headed serpent snaked its way to the very top. They weren't real of course, but to be honest, Jess thought they looked a tiny bit scary. It made her nervous even though they were just stone.

"We have to walk up *that*?" Jess asked.

Her mom gave her "the look." And she decided to start climbing.

As she hiked up the steps, beads of sweat formed on the back of her neck. She couldn't believe how HOT it was. In Boston, it was definitely not hot

"Wat" Could It Be?

in February, Jess thought.

"I thought this was supposed to be the end of the cool season," Jess complained to her mom. "If it's *this* hot during the *cool* season, how hot is it during the *hot* season?"

"Hotter," she replied curtly.

Finally, Jess dragged herself up the last few steps to the temple.

And it *was* really, really beautiful. In fact, it took away any breath that Jess had left. Gold gleamed everywhere. A fence with gold and red spear-like posts protected a golden pyramid tower in the center of the temple. Golden Buddhas sat in different positions around the gate. The golden peaked roofs of the temple buildings glittered around them. Tourists wandered around taking pictures. A few people knelt with their heads bowed in front of the golden Buddhas.

"That's the pagoda," Nong May said. She smiled

wide. "See? *Suay*." Beautiful. She pointed to the golden tower. "It holds an ancient relic."

"Ancient relic?"

"Yes, people believe it has great powers. Over 500 years ago the King ordered the relic to be put on the back of a white elephant. The elephant ran through the jungle and up the mountain to this spot. Here he turned around three times and trumpeted. Sadly, he died. But the King thought this was a sign and ordered the golden pagoda to be built here to keep the relic safe."

"That is really sad about the elephant, but I guess he did his job," Jess said. "Chiang Mai has a lot of history."

"What kind of history do you have in Boston?" Nong May asked.

Jess had to think a minute.

"Boston is one of the oldest cities in the United States, but it doesn't have as much history as this."

Jess thought some more.

"Well, I guess we do have history, but it is much different than yours. We did have the Boston Tea Party and Paul Revere. Boston is the place where America started its fight for freedom from the British. That was over two hundred years ago." It was cool that she could share some history from her own city with her new friend.

As they strolled around the pagoda, Nong May snuck the drawing out of her backpack. "Let's find some people to ask," she whispered. She glanced back at her mother.

The girls ran ahead of their mothers. They asked the man at the souvenir shop. He did not know. Then they asked the woman at the snack bar. She did not know. Next they asked a group of people who had stopped to look at the white elephant statue. They definitely did not know. They were just tourists from Austria (not Australia).

"Wat" Could It Be?

Jess saw some people in orange robes. They looked important. So she grabbed the drawing from Nong May and ran up to them.

"Have you seen this golden temple? Do you know where it is?" Jess asked.

"Jess, no!" Nong May ran up behind Jess. "They are monks, spiritual people here to study. You should not disturb—"

One of the men in the orange robes raised his hand slowly to quiet Nong May.

"It is no problem," he said in English. "Let me see."

The monk looked carefully at the drawing. His face showed a quick look of surprise. Just as quickly, his face grew peaceful again.

The monk spoke rapidly to Nong May in Thai.

"Khop khun kha." Nong May thanked the monk and brought her palms together in her heart center. Her hands tilted outward as she bowed her head lower. Her thumbs touched between her eyebrows this time. The monk turned to catch up to the others on their way to evening chant.

"What did he say?" Jess asked.

"He said maybe it is just a drawing. Or maybe not. He said they have heard of a lost golden temple in the jungle of the Mae Sa Valley. But no one has ever found it."

Nong May looked like she had just lost her favorite stuffed animal. "If the monks of *Doi Suthep* don't know of this golden temple, then nobody will," she said without her usual smile. Now Jess looked like she had lost Pink Dog, *her* favorite stuffed animal.

The moms rounded the corner just as Nong May was tucking the drawing safely back into her backpack.

"Where have you girls been?" Khun Mali asked.

"Jess wanted to see the souvenirs, so we ran ahead. *Khor toht kha*," Nong May said. She looked at her feet.

"I'm sorry too," Jess said. She also looked down at *her* feet.

"Well, girls. We do need to get back. Come along," Mrs. Johnson said.

As they walked down the stairs through the trees, they could hear the monks chanting in the distance. Their voices vibrated down the mountain. It gave Jess an eerie but somehow calm feeling. It sounded to her like they were chanting to find the golden temple.

Chapter 6

The Map

The next day Jess and Nong May played and played. They snuck around the hanging orchid plants during hide and seek at the orchid farm. They ran through the grass and blooming flowers in a game of tag at the Thai Garden Guesthouse. Jess had to stop and smell a few flowers now and then, but she made sure not to get caught when she did. And when they were tired of running, they got out their famous singing dolls again. Madee and Gina had now become winners of *Thailand's Got Talent* and *America's Got Talent* TV shows.

After a long, long, looonnnggg day of playing, they were really, really, reallllyyy hungry for dinner. Khun Mali had prepared a special meal for the Johnsons. Nong May was anxious for Jess to try her favorite homemade Thai food. And Jess could barely wait.

Once they were seated for dinner, Jess did her very best to be polite. She wanted to gobble down every bit of food on the table to feed her growling tummy. But she knew her mom would kill her if she didn't show good manners.

"Over here is *khao soi*. This is very popular here in Chiang Mai," Nong May's older brother, Pee Aran, said. He described all the foods to the Johnsons.

The flat, yellow noodles and chicken covered in a coconut curry sauce looked *and* smelled delicious to Jess. Crispy, fried noodles layered the top. Now Jess' tummy growled even louder.

"And over here is *som tam*. It is a salad. We mix green papaya with tomatoes, spicy Thai chilies, beans, garlic, small dried shrimp, a little fish sauce, lime juice, palm sugar, and peanuts," Pee Aran continued.

Jess tried not to scrunch up her nose, but she thought that sounded like a weird mix of stuff. Really? Dried shrimp and papaya? Mixed together? Definitely weird. Then she remembered her mom say that food in another country is not "weird," it is just "different." Jess still wasn't sure about this one. But she guessed she would just have to be polite and give it a try.

"And this one you might know? *Pad thai?* But I am sure it will taste different from what you eat in America. Much better. We made it so you can taste the difference," Pee Aran said. He smiled.

Jess' parents liked Thai food, so they often ordered *pad thai* on a Friday night at home. She loved the Thai stir-fried noodles. She couldn't wait to see how it tasted in the place it was really from.

The Map

"And this one is my favorite," Nong May spoke. "It is *khao niaow ma muang*. It is a sweet sticky rice with mango. We eat this for dessert, mostly in April and May because that's when mangos are in season. But we made this one special for you."

Jess took a sip of the grape juice Nong May gave her and watched her parents. She copied how they dished out and ate their food. They started with a small serving of sticky rice. Then they tried a small serving of each dish, one at a time. When they finished, they refilled their plates with another small serving. The food was sooooooo good. But the servings seemed *really* small compared to how Jess was used to serving herself in America. Jess felt like a pig each time she went back for more, but that is what everyone did. She thought her servings of the rice and mango dessert were *especially* small, so she kept going back for more until her mom gave her "the look."

After they had eaten all they could and Jess'

stomach no longer growled, the parents excused the kids to play outside on the porch. Jess hopped into the nearby rocking chair. She carefully put what was left of her grape juice down on the floor beside her.

Off to the side, Jared and Pee Aran compared their karate and Thai boxing moves. Nong May knelt next to Jess. She unfolded the picture of the golden temple and spread it out on the porch floor.

"I wonder where this could be," she said under her breath.

Jess leaned forward in her rocking chair. "Maybe we could ask Khun Yaa. She might—"

"Hi-ya!" Jared yelled loudly. He turned around and jabbed his foot in the air. His foot crashed into Jess' rocking chair. Her chair spun around. The bottom of the rocker hit her glass. Spin. Spinn. Spinnn. The bottom of the glass was spinning around on its edges, ready to fall over at any moment. Jess lunged out of her chair to grab the glass. CRASH. She was a second too late. Grape juice spilled everywhere. *Everywhere.* Even all over the picture of the golden temple.

"Oh no! Not again," Jess cried.

Everyone stopped and looked at the mess on the floor. Jared made one of his "oh no, don't tell mom" looks. Pee Aran acted like it was his fault and went in to get a towel to clean it up. And Nong May covered a tiny laugh with her hand. Jess had no idea what was so funny. She had just ruined her friend's picture. She felt terrible. Again.

51

"It is okay," Nong May said smiling.

"I'm sorry," Jess said. "Bad luck seems to be following me on this trip."

"*Mai pen rai.* No problem, Jess. Really, is—wait." Nong May looked puzzled. "What . . . ? What is this?" Blurred lines started to appear on top of the picture of the golden temple.

"Look at this. It looks like another drawing is showing up on top of the picture." Nong May shifted the picture around.

"Maybe it's a magic trick," Jared said.

"Maybe it is a secret code left behind by some smugglers," Pee Aran chimed in. He peered over Nong May's shoulder, a towel in his hand.

Jess sighed. She was upset about spilling the juice. "Maybe it's a piece of paper that has grape juice all over it."

"Maybe it is—Jess, it is a secret map. I think your bad luck is really *good* luck!" Nong May said excitedly.

The Map

Jess peered over Nong May's shoulder at the map.

"You're right, it does look like a map. Hmmmmm. I wonder who wrote this map. Where do you think it leads?" Jess asked.

"Look. Down here on the right," Nong May pointed. "That looks like it could be the golden temple. Maybe it leads there."

"The golden temple?" Jared and Pee Aran asked at the same time.

"What are you two talking about?" Jared asked.

The girls looked at each other. Nong May nodded to her.

"I broke a Buddha at Khun Yaa's house," Jess admitted.

"What?" Jared groaned. "Ohhhhh, Jess. What—"

"It is okay. There was a paper inside with a drawing of a *wat* on it," Nong May said.

"A what?" Jared asked.

"A temple," Pee Aran explained.

"Yes, a golden temple," Nong May said.

Jess continued the story. "So we went to *Doi Suthep* to see if we could find any clues about the golden temple."

"We talked to a lot of people. But they didn't know anything about it. Even the monks didn't know anything. Pee Aran, have you seen it before? Do *you* know where it is?" Nong May asked. She had hope in her voice.

"No. I do not know of such a thing," Pee Aran said. He studied the map. He scrunched his eyebrows together. "This looks like it could be the stream that runs in the jungle behind us. But I have not seen this trail. I am very sorry, but I do not know where this maps leads."

Jess stood up. She knew what they had to do. And it scared her. She took a deep breath. "There is only one way to find out," she said in her most courageous voice. "We need to follow this map."

Chapter 7

Elephants, Motorbikes, and Tigers

It sounded like a good plan. But the next morning Nong May and Pee Aran quickly figured out it was not a ten-minute walk or even a one-hour jungle trek. They would need another way to get there than just their feet. Luckily, Pee Aran had just the answer to their problem.

"Meet us at the Elephant Rescue Center at 3:00. Jared is coming with me again today. After we are done working there, we can borrow some motorbikes and follow the map," Pee Aran explained.

So Jess and Nong May waited. And waited. And waited. They didn't even want to play dolls. Or even eat. Jess' stomach was all tied up in knots. This waiting was going to kill her. Nong May's smiles were fewer and fewer the longer they waited.

"Maybe we should go over to the Elephant Rescue Center now. I can show you the elephants. You can feed them. At least the time will go by faster," Nong May suggested.

Anything. *Anything* would be better than waiting Jess thought. So they wandered down the road to the Elephant Rescue Center.

When they walked through the entrance, Jess' eyes grew wide.

"Whoa! This is AWE-SOME. I have never seen so many elephants roaming around. Not even at the zoo. What are the elephants rescued from?"

"Some people use the elephants to help them work. Other people use them to do shows and rides for tourists. To get them to do that, they have to break them from being a wild animal and train them to obey humans. This can really hurt them."

"That's sad," Jess said. She frowned.

"Yes. Here they can be wild animals again. When they first come to the center, they keep their trunks down. They seem very unhappy. But after the center takes

care of them, they wave their trunks high up in the air. You can see that they are happy again."

Nong May and Jess stood under the shelter of a large open-aired hut with a thatched roof. They fed the elephants mushy bananas, papayas, and rice balls. Jess couldn't believe she was really in Thailand feeding elephants. This would be the *best* story to tell her friends back home in Boston. She had so much fun she forgot about the time.

"On no! It's 3:15. We need to find our brothers," Nong May said.

Nong May and Jess hurried over to meet their brothers. Pee Aran was busy showing Jared how to use the motorbike. Jared had used a dirt bike on some of their summer trips in New Hampshire, so Jess was pretty sure he knew what to do. But to be honest, she was still a little anxious. This was NOT New Hampshire.

"Are you girls ready to go?" Jared asked.

"Yup. We studied the map this morning. We're good to go," Jess said. She tried to hide her nervousness, but she felt shaky inside.

Jess hopped on the back of Jared's motorbike. As he zipped out of the Elephant Rescue Center, she hung on to him for dear life. Jared was clearly going a little slower than Pee Aran, but it still felt faster than Jess would have liked. She didn't want to admit it, but riding off into the jungle of Thailand was a teensy weensy bit more scary than riding

on the back of her dad's dirt bike in New Hampshire.

As they zoomed down the double-track jungle road, they turned left and then right. And then they turned right and then left again. Or maybe it was right? Jess hoped Nong May and Pee Aran knew where they were going. She had already lost track.

They rode for about 20 minutes. Jared and Jess began to fall farther and farther behind Pee Aran and Nong May. Then all of a sudden, they stopped.

"What's wrong?" Jess asked. Her eyebrows furrowed with worry.

Jared sighed. "I think I've got a flat tire."

Jess' stomach dropped all the way to the ground. How were they going to find the golden temple? Forget that. How were they going to get out of the jungle before it was dark and wild animals went on the prowl? Her heart skipped a beat. Weren't there tigers in Thailand? Tigers with sharp claws?

BIG sharp claws . . .

Chapter 8

The Jungle Trek

Pee Aran and Nong May circled back to Jared and Jess. Minutes later, Pee Aran raced off to find a new tire. Jared, Jess, and Nong May waited on the side of the dusty jungle road. So far, Jess hadn't seen a single tiger. But it was still light out. Right now, she didn't mind the heat of the afternoon sun shining down on them. But it was only a matter of time before the sun went down, Jess thought to herself.

Nong May didn't seem at all bothered by the

awful situation they were in. She pulled the map out of her pack and concentrated hard on it.

"We are not that far from the small trail that leads to the end. See?" Nong May said. She pointed at a faint line on the map. "I think we should walk down this way."

Jess raised her eyebrows. She wasn't too sure this was a good idea. Walking through the jungle? Alone? In Thailand? With tigers?

"Jess, come on," Nong May said with a smile. "I trek through the jungle all the time. We will be just fine."

Just fine. Right. Especially with all this bad luck happening lately. Jess *really* wasn't sure about this. But she did not want to be embarrassed in front of her friend. And she did not want to embarrass her friend by not agreeing to her idea. Her dad told her that in Thailand, you have to be careful to "save face." This meant not embarrassing yourself or others. Her dad said maybe *that* was one reason the Thai people smile a lot.

Wait a minute, Jess thought. Maybe that was why Nong May smiled and giggled so much. Now it was starting to make sense.

"Okay, let's go," Jess said. Not feeling very brave, she gave Nong May her best fake smile.

"Wait a minute," Jared said. "Where do you think you are going?"

"We are just going down the road to look for the trail. I trek in the jungle all the time. We will be just fine," Nong May said.

"We won't go very far," Jess added. But she still wasn't too sure how fine they would be.

"Okay," Jared sighed. "But seriously, don't go too far."

The heat of the day gave the blue sky a hazy look. The rounded green mountains and hillsides reminded Jess of the mountains she saw on her summer trips in New Hampshire. But the thick trees were more tangled together. You could not see where one stopped and one started. It made the jungle look darker and scarier than the forests of New Hampshire.

Nong May grabbed two long branches and pulled the twigs and leaves off. Birds twittered away as the girls hiked with their makeshift walking sticks.

Nong May started to make up a Thai song to go with all the music the birds were making. "I'm not such a good singer even though I like to sing," Nong May said as she giggled and covered her mouth.

Jess didn't want her new friend to be embarrassed, but she didn't know the Thai words to sing along. So she decided to beatbox along with her. Nong May thought that was really funny. And the two girls laughed even harder.

As they rounded the fourth curve of the dirt road, Nong May looked at the map again. "The trail should be right around here."

The Jungle Trek

"I don't see any path," Jess said. She looked on both sides of the old dirt road.

"Over here," Nong May called. "It looks like this could be a trail."

"Are you sure this isn't a deer path?" Did they even have deer in Thailand? Jess didn't know. Either way, it didn't look like a trail that was well traveled by people who could find them if they got lost.

"Come on. Let's go." Nong May said. She used her arms to push aside huge leaves of the tall bushes that grew over the trail. She stepped into the jungle. The bushes closed behind her like they were eating her up.

With her heart beating fast, Jess took a gulp, pushed the bushes aside, and followed behind.

Skinny tree trunks had fallen down this way and that all along the tiny, twisting path through the jungle. Spooky looking moss-covered rocks jutted out into the trail here and there. Jess wondered what kind of snakes lurked under all the leaves. She didn't look under them to find out though. The trees grew so close together they almost blocked out the sun entirely. Jess' heart beat faster. Was the sun setting already?

Something rustled in the bushes. Jess whipped around but couldn't see anything through the leaf-covered ground. Was it a snake? A tiger? Her imagination?

Jess gasped. "Did you hear that?"

"Yes," Nong May said. She looked a little more worried now. "But I am sure it is all fine." She offered a small smile but walked a little faster.

Jess kept looking behind her as they walked. It was quiet except for the rustling sound that seemed to keep following them. Where were the singing birds when you needed them?

Ahead, Nong May pushed back some more bushes to reveal a stream. The water flowed gently, a little too wide and a little too deep to cross. They were trapped. The rustling sound would catch up to them if they didn't find a way across.

"Look. Over there," Nong May said and pointed. "We can cross on the log."

Jess watched Nong May glide across.

Then she started to cross, one foot in front of the other. She focused her attention on her feet. Right foot. Left foot. She really did not want to get wet. The noise rustled closer. Jess moved faster. Right foot. Left foot. Right. Left. Right. Left.

"Whoa!" Jess shouted. Her foot slipped off the mossy log. "Whoa!" She caught her balance at the last moment and then skipped, hopped, and ran across the rest of the log to the other side.

"Phew! That was scary."

Nong May covered her mouth and giggled again.

Jess knew that she was embarrassed for her, so she smiled and giggled too.

"Now, where is the path?" Nong May wondered aloud.

Jess breathed easier on the other side of the stream across from the scary rustling sound. She really, really, really hoped they didn't lose the path because she really, really, really didn't want to be lost in the jungle all night.

With the snakes.

And the tigers.

And who knew what else. She quickly started to pull back the bushes and search.

"Ouch!" Jess said. She tripped over some twisty roots and fell to the ground.

"Are you okay?" Nong May asked.

"Yeah. I'm good. Let's just find this path and get out of here. Maybe we should turn around before it gets dark?"

"No, no. We are fine. We have lots of time. I know we are almost there. I can feel it. We just need to find where the path is."

"Yup, okay. We're fine. Always fine," Jess said under her breath. She leaned over to push some bushes aside. Wait. Something was wrong. Something was missing. Nothing hit her chin when she bent over.

"Oh no, where's my soccer necklace?" Jess asked. Her heart beat faster. It wasn't hanging on her neck anymore. This trip really *was* bad luck.

"You lost your necklace? *Khor toht kha.* I am so sorry. Maybe it came off when you fell?"

The girls scrambled back to where Jess had fallen.

Nong May could see why Jess had fallen. Twisty roots covered the ground. Leafy bushes, moss, and lush vines climbed the hillside. She followed the vines with her eyes. Up, up, up they went. Towards the top, a sparkle caught her eye. Sunlight glinted off what looked like a small spot of gold behind the vines.

"Wait a minute. This isn't *just* a hillside." Nong May froze. She started pulling back the leaves and vines from the hillside as fast as she could.

"Nong May, what are you doing? I don't think I lost my necklace there."

"No. Your necklace isn't here." Nong May pulled away another vine and took a deep breath. "But I think we found the golden temple."

Chapter 9

The Golden Temple

"The golden temple. This is it. See the gold up there?" Nong May pointed at the plant-covered hillside above them.

Sure enough, the sun glinted off some gold beneath the leafy vines.

"The golden temple," Jess said. She caught her breath. "Only the gold is all covered up by the jungle. It looks like it was built into this hillside." Jess worked faster now.

"Be careful of snakes," Nong May said. "Don't move too quickly."

"For real?" Jess squeaked. She had hoped she just imagined the snakes. They were real? Yikes.

"Yes. Watch where you put your hands."

Just as Nong May said that, a snake slithered out right by Jess' foot.

"Ack!" Jess yelled. She jumped what seemed like ten feet off the ground. "I'm done here. I hate snakes." They were way too real now.

"No, no," Nong May said. She shook her head. "That snake is fine. No poison. We must keep going." Nong May reached over and cleared another vine away.

No poison? So everything was fine? What if the next one was poisonous? Jess' stomach flipped upside down. She stood there watching Nong May clear away the leaves and vines. She really did not want to "lose face" with Nong May. So she found

The Golden Temple

every last ounce of courage she had inside her. She looked first. And then, after she looked very, very carefully, she pulled away the leaves and vines.

"I think I found something." Nong May waved her hands and shouted.

Jess turned and saw a small wooden door peeking through the leaves. Gold and black swirls decorated the edges of the door. They framed a golden Buddha whose hands pressed together at heart center.

Nong May pushed the door. It didn't budge. Jess joined in. Push. Push. Push. The girls slammed their bodies against the old wood. The door creaked open.

"Whoa. It's dark in here," Jess said.

Small cracks of light glowed through a leaf-covered opening off to the right. Spider webs wrapped the corners of the room. Jess was sure she could hear the spiders scurry away from the light shining through the door behind them. She shivered.

The Golden Temple

"I don't think anyone has been here in a long time," Nong May said as she stepped onto the dark red floor inside the small temple.

A large golden Buddha sat crossed-legged on an altar in front of them. Lots of other small golden Buddhas and old relics rested below. Two large columns decorated in gold and black swirls rose up to the ceiling on either side of the altar. Yellow drapes, pale from dust, hung from the walls. Underneath the dust, a hint of gold peeked through.

"Watch your step, Nong May," Jess whispered. "You said there may be snakes, and I totally think there are spiders."

"I do not like spiders at all," Nong May said. She shuddered.

"Me either," Jess said. "I think I hate them more than snakes."

The two girls held on to each other as they walked towards the altar. The farther they walked inside, the more the darkness seemed to surround them.

Suddenly the door creaked behind them.

Jess spun around just in time to see it swing shut.

They were trapped.

"Ack!" Jess screamed.

"Jaak!" Nong May screamed.

The girls stumbled through near darkness towards the door.

"Oy!" Ouch. Nong May said in pain as she fell to the floor.

"Nong May, are you okay?" Jess asked. "Where are you? What happened?"

"I am over here. I tripped over something. I can't see."

"Don't worry. We are going to be just fine," Jess said. Just fine. This time, they *would* be just fine. She would make sure of it.

Jess reached for the door, yanked hard, and flung

it open. The sunlight streamed in.

Nong May was on her knees. She squinted at Jess, the light from the open door in her eyes. A wooden box with gold latches lay open next to her. Pictures, statues, and papers spilled out on to the floor.

Jess ran over to help her up. "What is all this?" she asked.

Nong May looked down at the box and its contents scattered all over the floor. She caught her breath and her eyes opened wide in shock.

"It is our *Phra Somdej* amulet!"

Chapter 10

Good Luck Again

Good luck. Good luck. Good luck! The girls jumped up and down in a circle, hugging each other. They found the *Phra Somdej* amulet.

"Come on. Let's bring it back to your family now," Jess said. She took a few steps towards the door. She felt happy to find the amulet. But the anxiety of being in the creepy jungle gnawed at her stomach.

"But the box—there are more things here,"

Good Luck Again

Nong May said. "We can't just leave it. Maybe it belongs to our family or other families in the valley. I wonder if the robbers left our stuff here and then forgot or got caught?"

"But we can't really carry it back on the motorbikes. It's too big and heavy," Jess replied. She stepped closer towards the door. "You have to come back and show your family the temple anyway, right? Let's hide it in a safe spot for now."

Nong May nodded.

They quickly packed everything back in the box, except the amulet.

"Here. Let's push it over here." Jess pointed behind a curtain.

They arranged the curtain so no one could see the box. The girls ran out of the temple. Nong May held the amulet tightly in her hand. Jess grabbed some gigantic leaves to place over the door to hide it, too.

Then the girls raced across the stream without falling. They raced through the overgrown leafy bushes pushing them to the side of the twisty path. And they raced all the way down the windy jungle road. The girls reached Pee Aran and Jared just as the boys finished changing the tire on Jared's bike.

"We found it!" Nong May blurted out to Pee Aran.

"The map, the path, led to—" Jess started.

"—the golden temple." Nong May finished.

Breathless from running, the girls' words tumbled out in short bursts.

"Snakes and spiders . . ."

"The door slammed shut. We couldn't see . . ."

"But then the amulet was on the floor . . ."

Pee Aran and Jared stared at the girls. Their eyes grew wide. They looked at each other. Then they looked back at the girls again.

"What's going on?" Pee Aran asked.

Good Luck Again

"Back home. Now. Please." Jess said urgently.

"We've found the *Phra Somdej*!" Nong May turned to Pee Aran. *"Garunaa."* Please.

Pee Aran nodded. "Okay then. We go." The girls hopped on the back of the motorbikes and they sped off down the jungle road.

Forever later, they squealed to a stop outside of Nong May's house. The bikes had barely stopped when the girls jumped off. They ran inside as fast as they could to tell their moms about the golden temple and the mystery they had just solved.

At dinner that night, they repeated the story they had told their moms.

"So the amulet must have fallen out of the box onto the floor. Can you believe it?" Nong May finished telling her grandmother in Thai. She held up the amulet to show her.

Khun Yaa smiled wide. Her eyes sparkled. She spoke to Nong May for a few minutes. Her singsongy voice almost lulled Jess to sleep. It had been a long, eventful day after all. But then Nong May spoke up.

"She says that she thinks she knows what happened. She doesn't think it was the robbers. She thinks grandfather packed up some of our valuables that night before the robbers came. He brought them into the jungle to keep them from being stolen."

"But that doesn't explain the secret map," Jess said.

Good Luck Again

"Hmmmm." Nong May thought for second. Then she sing-songed a question to her grandmother.

"She says he must have made the map when he had found the golden temple so he could find it again. He hid it away to keep it safe."

"Did your grandmother know about the golden temple?" Jared asked.

Nong May asked her grandmother.

"She says he never mentioned the golden temple before. She thinks maybe he did not want to have tourists trekking up in the jungle behind us all the time. So he kept the golden temple a secret."

"But how did he make the map secret? Is that a magic trick of some sort?" Jess asked.

Khun Boon-Mee, Nong May's father, piped in. "I know how he did that. We did that as kids. You mix baking soda and water together like a paint. Then you can use a paintbrush to write your secret message. You can hold it up to a light bulb or put grape juice on it to read it."

"That's it! The map appeared after the grape juice spilled," Jess said. "I guess it wasn't bad luck after all."

"No. And I think good luck has returned to the Wattana family too," Khun Boon-Mee said with a smile. "I just received a call today. One of our customers doubled his order. He bought some of his orchids in Singapore. Now he has decided to buy all of his orchids from us."

"Wonderful! We heard some good news today too," Mrs. Johnson said. "The people we met in Chiang Mai are planning to donate money to the hill tribe village school."

Everyone smiled. It was a great night.

As Jess strolled back to the guesthouse with her family, she smiled to herself. What an awesome day. She didn't even mind so much that she had lost her favorite soccer necklace if it meant her new friend would be happy.

Jess put on her pajamas and brushed her teeth.

"I'm going to sleep like a rock tonight," she said to her mom. She lay her head down on the pillow. Jess closed her eyes, but she could feel something digging into her back. Argh. She hoped it wasn't a spider biting her.

Jess rummaged around her bed until her hand landed on something round and cool. She squinted in the darkness at the object. Her soccer necklace! She hadn't lost it after all. Maybe good luck would follow her on the rest of the trip. She wrapped her arms around Pink Dog and smiled to herself as her eyes slowly closed for the night.

The next morning, the sun shone brightly through the open windows. Jess stretched and smiled again. The success of yesterday bathed over her like the warm sun.

Nong May called at the door. "Jess, come on."

"Just a minute. I have to get dressed," Jess replied.

Jess quickly changed her clothes. She joined Nong May outside in the bright sun and lush, colorful grounds. They both looked forward to a day of playing. On the list was hide and seek, tag, and famous singing dolls, of course. But first, they needed some pretty orchids for their hair.

As they walked through the orchid farm looking for the perfect flower, one of the orchids caught Nong May's eye.

Good Luck Again

"Look! My grandfather's rare orchid. It is blooming again. It is *suay*, not *suay*," Nong May said varying her tone. Beautiful, not unlucky. "Good luck has for sure returned," Nong May said. She shared a warm Thai smile with Jess.

Jess hugged her new friend. "Everything is going to be *just fine*."

And this time, she knew it was true.

Sneak Peek of Another Adventure

Mystery of the Disappearing Dolphin

Chapter One

Nothing made sense.

Nothing.

Izzy watched the spooky shadow float into her stateroom. It swam through the air, diving and rising over her bed. With each dip, it crept closer and closer. She tried to scream to scare the shadow away. But no sound came out. She felt frozen in her bed. Her legs and arms wouldn't move.

She yelled again. And again, there was no noise.

Her heart pounded.

The gray shape shifted into something she knew.

A fish. A giant fish. A fish that purred like a cat.

Izzy couldn't figure out how the fish got inside Dream

Catcher, the sailboat she lived on. The silver monster drifted over her bed. It dove toward her again. Streaks of blue light flashed over its back.

Slowly, it swished its tail up and down, up and down. And then it twisted and flipped like a dolphin.

The dolphin squeaked at her in perfect English. "Don't worry. Be happy." It sang the words.

Izzy hadn't known dolphins could speak English or sing. She answered in Spanish. She didn't know what she said, but she knew she'd said it perfectly. Izzy loved that she knew more Spanish than the dolphin.

The dolphin chattered at her.

Clang, clang, clang.

It sounded like a metal baseball bat hitting the school's jungle gym. Kind of.

Clang, clang. Clang. Clang, clang.

Izzy opened her eyes.

Poof! The dolphin disappeared.

Izzy shook her head to clear it. Katie Kitty still

slept in her favorite spot. The cat lay between Izzy and the hull, or outside wall, of the boat.

What a weird dream.

Her heart still pounded. The dream seemed spooky real. She half expected the dolphin to float back into her stateroom.

Izzy heard the clanging again. Now she knew the sound. The wind must have picked up. The lines that raised the sails banged against the mast, the tall pole that held the main sail. Izzy tried to think of the word her dad used.

Halyards. That was it. That was the sailing word for them. The halyards clanged against the mast.

The wind rarely blew in the morning. A storm must be coming in. That never happened this time of year.

Weird dream.

Weird weather.

A weird start to the day.

Find out what happens to
Izzy and Patti in the
Pack-n-Go Girls book,
Mystery of the
Disappearing Dolphin.

Dive into More Reading Fun!

Take Another Trip to Thailand with Jess and Nong May!

Mystery of the Naga at Night

When Jess arrives to help Nong May at one of the hill tribe village schools in Thailand, Nong May is happier than ever to see her. For the last week, she's been scared stiff. Every night, she's seen the mythical seven-headed Naga serpent slithering through the village. And this Naga was not out to protect anyone. It had to be a bad dream. Or was it? *Coming soon!*

Discover Mexico with Izzy and Patti!

Mystery of the Thief in the Night

Nine-year-old Izzy Bennett can't wait to explore the pretty little Mexican village with her new friend Patti. Life is perfect. At least it's perfect until they realize there's a midnight thief on the loose! Don't miss the second Mexico book, *Mystery of the Disappearing Dolphin.*

Meet More Pack-n-Go Girls!

Discover Austria with Brooke and Eva!

Mystery of the Ballerina Ghost

Nine-year-old Brooke Mason is headed to Austria. She'll stay in Schloss Mueller, an ancient Austrian castle. Eva, the girl who lives in Schloss Mueller, is thrilled to meet Brooke. Unfortunately, the castle's ghost isn't quite so happy. Don't miss the second and third Austria books: *Mystery of the Secret Room* and *Mystery at the Christmas Market*.

Discover Brazil with Sofia and Júlia!

Mystery of the Troubled Toucan

Nine-year-old Sofia Diaz's world is coming apart. So is the rickety old boat that carries her far up the Rio Negro river in Brazil. Crocodiles swim in the dark waters. Spiders scurry up the

twisted tree trunks. And a crazy toucan screeches a warning. It chases Sofia and Júlia, her new friend, deep into the steamy rainforest. There they stumble upon a shocking discovery.

What to Know Before You Go!

Where is Thailand?

CHIANG MAI

BANGKOK

Thailand is located in Southeast Asia. To the north and east are the countries of Myanmar (also sometimes called Burma), Laos, and Cambodia. The long southern part of Thailand connects with Malaysia. The Gulf of Thailand and the Adaman Sea are on either side. Tourists often visit the city of Bangkok, the mountains in the northern part of Thailand, and the beach in the southern part of Thailand.

Some people say that Thailand is shaped like an elephant's head. The elephant has played an important role in Thai history. It is one of Thailand's national symbols.

Facts about Thailand

Official Name: Thailand was known as Siam until 1939. It is now officially the Kingdom of Thailand. Thailand means "land of the free."

Capital: Bangkok. Bangkok's full ceremonial name is Krungthepmahanakhon Amonrattanakosin Mahintharayutthaya Mahadilokphop Noppharatratchathaniburirom Udomratchaniwetmahasathan Amonphimanawatansathit Sakkathattiyawitsanukamprasit. That is the longest place name (with spaces) in the world.

Currency: Baht

Government: Thailand is a constitutional monarchy. The king is the leader of the country and very respected and loved. The country is governed by the prime minister, cabinet, and national assembly.

Language: Thai

Population: 69.52 million people (as of 2013 estimate)

Traveling in Thailand

Thailand is called the "land of smiles." And smiles will surely greet you. Traveling is fun and crazy. The streets are full of cars, taxis, tuk tuks (small three-wheeled, open-aired vehicles), songthaew (converted red pick-up trucks that are used as shared taxis), and motorbikes. They also drive on the left side of the road. So definitely be careful crossing the street. Look right, then left, then right again. And cross quickly!

What to Expect for Weather

The weather in Thailand is a tropical climate that is generally warm most of the year. The southern part of Thailand has only two seasons: rainy and dry. In the northern part of Thailand where Chiang Mai is located, there are three seasons: 1) the rainy season, which is from July to October; 2) the cool season, which is from November to February; and 3) the hot season, which is from March to June.

Thai Food

Thai food can be very spicy. In fact, it is so spicy that when you visit a Thai restaurant in the United States, they will ask you if you want your food mild, medium, hot, or Thai hot (meaning really, really spicy). At most Thai meals you will find rice, noodles, fish, shrimp, and soups. Northern Thailand is especially known for its Thai curries, which are different types of seafood, meats, and vegetables in a curry flavored sauce.

Recipe for Sticky Rice with Mango

Ingredients:

- 1 cup Thai sweet rice (also called sticky rice)
- 1-2 ripe mangos
- 4-5 tablespoons brown sugar or traditional Asian palm sugar
- ½ teaspoon salt
- 1 can good-quality coconut milk
- ½ teaspoon salt

Soak the rice in 1 cup of water for 20 minutes to 4 hours. Do not drain. Add ½ cup more water, ½ can coconut milk, ¼ teaspoon salt, and 1 tablespoon sugar. Bring to boil, partially cover, and reduce heat to medium-low. Simmer for 20 minutes or until coconut milk has been absorbed. Turn off heat and let sit for 5-10 minutes. For the sauce, warm the rest of the coconut milk over medium-low heat. Add 3 tablespoons of sugar. To serve, shape the rice into rectangles and triangles. Add cut up mango. Drizzle coconut sauce over the top. Garnish with fresh mint.

Say It in Thai!

English	Thai	Thai Pronunciation
Hello (woman/man)	สวัสดี	Sà-wàt-dee khâ/khráp
My name is (man/woman)	ผม/ดิฉันชื่อ	Phǒm/Dì-chǎn chêu khâ/khráp
Respectful title	คุณ	Khun
Younger sibling/people	น้อง	Nóng
Older sibling/people	พี่	Pêe
Please	กรุณา	Gà-rú-naa
Thank you (woman/man)	ขอบคุณ	Khòp khun khâ/khráp
Thank you/Thanks (to younger or friend)	ขอบใจ	Khòp jai
It's okay/Is no problem	ไม่เป็นไร	Mâi pen rai
You're welcome	ไม่เป็นไร	Mâi pen rai
My pleasure	ยินดี	Yin dee
I'm sorry/Excuse me	ขอโทษ	Khǒr tôht khâ/khráp
Temple	วัด	Wát
Awesome	เจ๋ง	Jěng

Tone Marker Note: There are five different tones in Thai: 1) low tone, which is flat at the bottom of the vocal range (hòk); 2) mid tone, which is flat at the middle of the vocal range (no marker is used); 3) falling tone, which starts high and falls sharply (mâi); 4) high tone, which is at the top of the vocal range (khráp); 5) rising tone, which starts low and rises gradually (sǎhm).

English	Thai	Thai Pronunciation
Beautiful/Unlucky	สวย/ซวย	Sŭay/Suay
Eeek!	จ๊าก	Jaak!
Ouch!	โอ๊ย	Ooy!
Yes	ใช่	Châi
No	ไม่	Mâi
0	ศูนย์	Sŏon
1	หนึ่ง	Nèung
2	สอง	Sŏrng
3	สาม	Săhm
4	สี่	Sèe
5	ห้า	Hâh
6	หก	Hòk
7	เจ็ด	Jèt
8	แปด	Bàat
9	เก้า	Gôw
10	สิบ	Sìp

Spelling Note: There are various systems for romanization of Thai. Some use transliteration while others use transcription to help with pronunciation. There is an official system from the Royal Thai General System of Transcription (RTGS). However, in practice, guides, websites, and dictionaries will differ, as will this glossary.

My Thailand Trip Planner

Where to go: _____

_____

_____

_____

_____

_____

_____

_____

_____

_____

_____

_____

_____

_____

What to do: _____

_____

_____

_____

_____

_____

_____

_____

_____

_____

_____

_____

_____

_____

_____

_____

My Thailand Trip Planner

My Thailand Trip Planner

Things I want to pack:

_____

_____

_____

_____

_____

_____

_____

_____

_____

_____

_____

_____

_____

Friends to send postcards to:

My Thailand Trip Planner

_____

_____

_____

_____

_____

_____

_____

_____

_____

_____

_____

_____

_____

Thank you to the following Pack-n-Go Girls:

Kylie Andrew
Sydney Marie Murphy
Sophie Ross
Skylar Stanley
Elana Sutton
Sarah Travis

Thank you also to Will Travis, the Colorado Springs Vistage gang, our friend Suki at Yakitori in Colorado Springs, Jasmine Andrew, Jeff and Montakran Schofield, and Jeannie Sheeks.

And a special thanks to my Pack-n-Go Girls co-founder,
Janelle Diller, and our husbands, Rich Travis and Steve Diller,
who have been along with us on this adventure.

 **Lisa Travis** has always dreamed of faraway places. Her childhood days of exploring old National Geographic magazines in her attic led her to the world beyond. She studied in Germany, traveled the USA in a Volkswagen camper, and lived and worked in South Korea. She currently finds ways to pack and go by designing global leadership programs. Her experiences around the world inspired her to write Pack-n-Go Girls stories that deliver positive messages around independence, adventure, and global awareness. Lisa lives, bikes, and skis in Colorado with her husband, two kids, and two dogs.

Adam Turner has been working as a freelance illustrator since 1987. He has illustrated coloring books, puzzle books, magazine articles, game packaging, and children's books. He's loved to draw ever since he picked up his first pencil as a toddler. Instead of doing the usual two-year-old thing of chewing on it or poking his eye out with  it, he actually put it on paper and thus began the journey. Adam also has had some crazy adventures. He's swum with crocodiles in the Zambezi, jumped out of a perfectly good airplane, and even fished for piranha in the Amazon. It's a good thing drawing relaxes his nerves! Adam lives in Arizona with his wife and their daughter.

Pack-n-Go Girls Online

Dying to know when the next Pack-n-Go Girls book will be out? Want to learn more Thai? Trying to figure out what to pack for your next trip? Looking for cool family travel tips? Interested in some fun learning activities about Thailand to use at home or at school while you are reading *Mystery of the Golden Temple*?

- Check out our website:
  www.packngogirls.com
- Follow us on Twitter:
  @packngogirls
- Like us on Facebook:
  facebook.com/packngogirls